Dear Parent:
Your child's love of reading starts here!

Every child learns to read in a different way and at his or her own speed. Some go back and forth between reading levels and read favorite books again and again. Others read through each level in order. You can help your young reader improve and become more confident by encouraging his or her own interests and abilities. From books your child reads with you to the first books he or she reads alone, there are I Can Read Books for every stage of reading:

SHARED READING
Basic language, word repetition, and whimsical illustrations, ideal for sharing with your emergent reader

BEGINNING READING
Short sentences, familiar words, and simple concepts for children eager to read on their own

READING WITH HELP
Engaging stories, longer sentences, and language play for developing readers

READING ALONE
Complex plots, challenging vocabulary, and high-interest topics for the independent reader

I Can Read Books have introduced children to the joy of reading since 1957. Featuring award-winning authors and illustrators and a fabulous cast of beloved characters, I Can Read Books set the standard for beginning readers.

A lifetime of discovery begins with the magical words **"I Can Read!"**

Visit www.icanread.com for information
on enriching your child's reading experience.

Library of Congress Control Number: 2021936534
ISBN 978-0-06-304092-2

21 22 23 24 25 LSCC 10 9 8 7 6 5 4 3 2 1
❖
First Edition

SHARED
READING

My First

I Can Read!

pinkfong

BABY SHARK™

Little Fish Lost

HARPER

An Imprint of HarperCollinsPublishers

Baby Shark wants to play.
But there is no one
to play with.

Baby Shark hears a sound.
"What was that?" he says.

Baby Shark finds a fish.

"Boo-hoo!" the fish says.

"I am lost."

"What happened?"
Baby Shark asks.
"A wave swept me away
from my reef," the fish says.

"It's easy to find a big reef.
We can see it from the sky,"
says Baby Shark.

"How am I going to get up
to the sky?" the fish says.
Baby Shark knows what to do.

Baby Shark finds a seesaw.

A seesaw goes up high!

A seesaw could go to the sky.

The seesaw goes up.

The fish jumps up.

The fish doesn't get up to the sky.

Baby Shark knows what to do.

Baby Shark swims off.
The fish follows him.

"Can you help,
Mr. Octopus?"
asks Baby Shark.

Mr. Octopus has long arms.

But he can't get up to the sky.

"I know!" Mr. Octopus says.
"Grandma Whale can help!"

Baby Shark swims off.

The fish follows.

The fish feels sad.
"Maybe I can't get up to
the sky."

"Don't give up!"
says Baby Shark.

23

The fish and Baby Shark
sing a song together.

"Baby Shark, doo-doo-doo-doo-doo-doo!"
The fish feels better.

Then they find
Grandma Whale!

Grandma Whale has
a blowhole.
She can spray way up high.

"Hold tight! Here we go!"
says Grandma Whale.
Baby Shark and the fish
get up to the sky!

"There!" the fish shouts.
"I see the reef!"

The fish splashes back down
into the water.
"Follow me!" the fish says.
He leads Baby Shark
to the big reef.

The fish is home.
Baby Shark is happy.
"Thank you, Baby Shark!"